It's a Crazy Day at the Zoo

Written by Stacy Lee Doyle
Illustrated by Bonnie Lemaire

ISBN: 978-1-7331738-2-7

To my beautiful grandchildren
Allie & Lila, who fill my heart with joy.

And to the grandchildren I haven't met yet.
I love you already.

This book belongs to..

I went to the zoo, and what did I see?

I saw a silly, little monkey, looking at me.

I scratched my head,

and he scratched his too.

I wonder what else that monkey can do.

I went over to the giraffes,
and what did I see?

I saw a **tall** giraffe, taller than a tree.

I looked up at him, and he looked down at me.

I wonder what all that giraffe can see.

I went over to the elephants,
and what did I see?
I saw the biggest creature
that I ever did see.

I went over to the lions,

and what did I see?

I saw the meanest lion that there ever could be.

I growled at him, but he **smiled** at me.

I wonder what that lion thought of me.

I went over to the rhinoceros, and what did I see?

I saw the strangest creature that I ever did see.

I said, "Mr. Rhino, can I give you a hug?"

I think he replied,

I went over to the koala bears,

and what did I see?

I saw the sweetest bear, sitting quietly.

I **waved** at him,

and he **waved** at me.

Good golly, oh gee!
He's so **fuzzy.**

I went over to the zebras, and what did I see?

I saw the coolest zebra that I ever did see.

I asked the zebra if I could have a ride.
"Sure, hop on!" I think he replied.

I went over to the seals, and what did I see?

I saw three seals, swimming happily.

I **clapped** my hands, and they **clapped** theirs too.
I wonder what else these seals can do.

I went over to the kangaroos, and what did I see?

I saw a momma kangaroo, and her baby Joey.

I asked, "Mrs. Kangaroo, can I hop in too?"

"Sure," she replied,

"but you must take off your shoes."

Kangaroos

I went over to the tigers and what did I see?

I saw the biggest cat that there ever could be.

I **lunged** towards the tiger,

then he **lunged** towards me.

TIGER

Good golly, oh gee!
He's so **scary.**

I went over to the hyenas, and what did I see?
I saw the **funniest** animals that I ever did see.

I **laughed** at them, and they **laughed** at me.
I wonder what they thought that was so funny.

I went over to the alligators, and what did I see?

I saw a hungry gator just staring at me.

SNAP! SNAP! SNAP! SNAP!

Good golly, oh gee!

I looked at my grandma, and she looked at me.

And we both decided that it's time to **flee.**

Made in the USA
Coppell, TX
09 November 2019

11156021R00021